Stop!

Before you turn the page —
take a piece of paper.
Pick up your pencil.
Draw a big triangle.

At the top point of the triangle write **Secret Government UFO Test Base**. At the left point write, **Dinosaur Graveyard**. At the right point, **Humongous Horror Movie Studios**. And in the exact center of the triangle write **Grover's Mill**.

Ah, Grover's Mill. A perfectly normal town, bustling with shops, gas stations, motels, restaurants, and schools. A small town with a great big heart, nestled snugly in the midst of —

Wait! Did we say *normal*? A studio where they film the cheapest horror movies ever made? The world's largest and smelliest graveyard of ancient dinosaur bones? A secret army base filled with captured alien spacecraft?

All this makes poor Grover's Mill the exact center of supreme intergalactic weirdness!

Turn the page.
If you dare.
Enter The Weird Zone!

COSMIC BOY VERSUS MEZMO HEAD!

THE WEIRD ZONE

COSMIC BOY VERSUS MEZMO HEAD!

by Tony Abbott

Cover illustration by Broeck Steadman
Illustrated by Lori Savastano

A
LITTLE APPLE
PAPERBACK

ISBN 0-590-67439-0

Text copyright © 1997 by Robert Abbott. Illustrations copyright © 1997 by Scholastic Inc. All rights reserved. Published by Scholastic Inc. LITTLE APPLE PAPERBACKS and the LITTLE APPLE logo are trademarks of Scholastic Inc.

12 11 10 9 8 7 6 5 4 3 2 1   7 8 9/9 0 1 2/0

Printed in the U.S.A.   40

First Scholastic printing, May 1997

To Dolores, for her never-ending faith

Contents

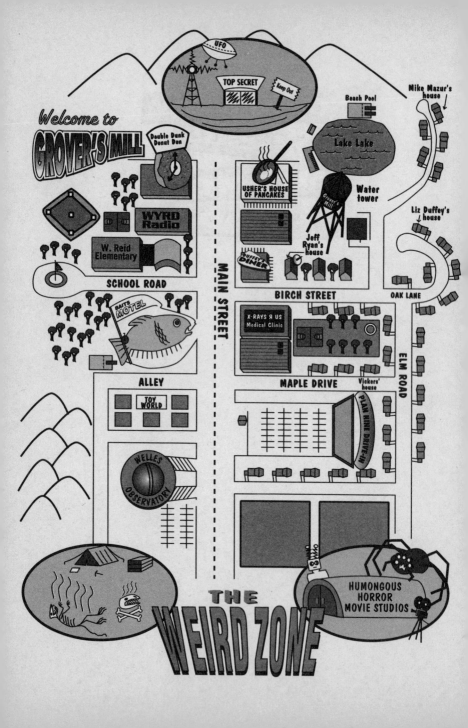

Zwhrrrr — rrrrr!

Jeff Ryan walked slowly backward out his front door. The big white satellite dish on his roof was spinning like crazy.

"Something's going on," Jeff mumbled to himself. He shifted a brightly colored box that he was holding in his arms.

Errrkk! An army truck screeched to a stop in his driveway and a bunch of men in army uniforms jumped out. They carried a small wooden crate to the house.

"Something *big* is going on!" Jeff whispered.

Jeff's mother, who was also dressed in an army uniform, and his father, who

1

puffed on a pipe, met the soldiers in the doorway.

Jeff heard only a few words of what they were saying. " . . . Last night . . . fell from the sky . . . top secret . . . global invasion . . . like a cabbage."

"Cabbage?" Jeff repeated to himself. "The army delivers vegetables now?"

A moment later, the soldiers climbed back into the truck and sped off. Jeff's parents carried the small crate inside.

"Bye-bye, sweetheart!" Mrs. Ryan called from the doorway. She blew Jeff a kiss.

For years, his parents had told him that the top-secret, high-security, fenced-in area north of Grover's Mill where his mother worked was really a shoe store.

But Jeff knew it wasn't. It was an army base. His friends said the army captured alien junk and did things with it there. Jeff wasn't sure if that was strange, or just normal everyday parent stuff.

Except that normal everyday stuff didn't seem to happen in Grover's Mill. That's why his friends called their town The Weird Zone.

"The center of intergalactic weirdness," Jeff mumbled, stepping to the sidewalk. "The Zone. A place where all the grown-ups are Zoners."

Bong! The giant donut-shaped clock on top of the Double Dunk Donut Den chimed the hour.

Sssss! The oversized pancake pan on Usher's House of Pancakes hissed out a cloud of smoke.

Jeff smiled. Those two restaurants had been bonging and hissing the hours for as long as he could remember.

Bweeeep! A high-pitched sound screeched through the air.

Jeff frowned. "That's a new one." He turned to see a man crouching in the bushes across the street. The man seemed to be holding a large leafy green thing in front of his face as a disguise. And he wore green shoes.

The instant he saw Jeff, the man slipped

back between the bushes and disappeared.

"Well, okay. That's a little strange." Jeff shifted the box and walked to the center of Grover's Mill. He stopped in front of the X-Rays Я Us Medical Clinic to wait for his best friend, Sean Vickers.

They walked to school together almost every day.

And today was special. The W. Reid Elementary School annual play tryouts were that morning. Jeff's teacher, Mrs. Carbonese, was directing an outer-space version of *The Wizard of Oz.* Jeff and his friends were going to try out.

The box Jeff was bringing had part of the Wizard's costume in it.

Jeff crouched and opened the box. It was his favorite toy a few years ago — a Cosmic Boy Space Helmet. It was based on the old TV show about a boy with incredible powers. Jeff was way beyond toys and shows like that now.

He pulled out the gray plastic bowl-shaped helmet with knobs on it. It had a

row of tiny lights across the front and two antennas sticking up behind the ears.

"Pretty old, but still cool." Jeff put the helmet on his head. It was tight. The helmet was made for a much smaller head. He turned to look at himself in the window of X-Rays Я Us.

Blink! Bzzz! Whrrr! The lights across the forehead blinked off and on, a little buzzer on top buzzed, and the antennas began to whirl slowly.

"Whoa!" Jeff exclaimed. "It still works!"

"So, Cosmic Boy, we meet again!" came a deep and gravelly voice.

Jeff whirled in fear. Then he laughed. "Sean!"

Sean Vickers trotted up to him. "Excellent helmet!" He tapped Jeff's plastic head a couple of times. "I wonder who will get to play the Wiz — "

Zzzzzzt! A sudden buzzing sound came from inside the X-Rays Я Us Medical Clinic.

"The big machine!" said Sean. "They're using it!"

The two friends looked through the window at a huge complicated machine with tubes and lights and wires and shiny metal parts. Bending over the controls was a man in a white lab coat.

"That X-ray machine has awesome power," Sean whispered to Jeff. "It blasts nuclear energy right through people's heads!"

"Are you sure?" Jeff wrinkled his nose. "X-ray machines don't really work like that, do they?"

Sean shrugged. "That's what I've heard."

Jeff nodded. "It reminds me of the sounds coming from my dad's office when he works at home."

Sean turned to Jeff and frowned. "Have you ever actually seen that office, Jeff?"

"It's in the attic. He doesn't want me in there."

"A secret room in your house that makes noises?" said Sean. "Pretty zoney, Jeff.

Come on, let's go. We just have one short class, then tryouts!"

It was then that Jeff noticed the sign in the X-Rays Я Us window. It said, CLOSED FOR VACATION. SEE-THROUGH YOU LATER!

"Wait a second," Jeff said, grabbing Sean's arm and pointing to the sign. "If the clinic is supposed to be closed, then who's that guy using the machine?"

Sean's eyes widened as the man in the white coat continued to press buttons on the machine. The man still had his back to the boys.

"Ah, a mystery!" Sean whispered. He put his finger to his lips and tiptoed into the clinic. Jeff was right behind him.

Suddenly — *zzzzzt!* — the X-ray machine buzzed loudly, exploding with large sparks.

The room flashed with bright light.

"Whoa!" Sean shouted. "He's gonna zap us!" Sean turned to run just as the man in the white coat jumped away from the exploding sparks.

Bweeeep! came a screeching sound.

Jeff tried to move, but Sean slammed him hard and the man tumbled back into both of them.

WHAM — WHAM — WHAM!

The three people crashed into one another with the force of planets colliding!

"Whoooomph!" groaned Sean as he drove Jeff out through the door to the sidewalk.

In the instant before he dropped, Jeff turned to see the man holding a large green vegetable in front of his face.

"Weird! Cabbage!" Jeff cried out, as he — *umph!* — slammed to the ground, his plastic Cosmic Boy helmet crunching down hard.

"My head!" he groaned.

Then things went dark in that head.

*T*hump-thump-thump!

When Jeff opened his eyes, he was face-down on the sidewalk outside the X-Rays Я Us Medical Clinic.

His head throbbed. His ears throbbed. His eyes throbbed. *Thump-thump-thump!*

"Uhhhh!" Jeff groaned as he slid out from under Sean's legs and got up. "Oh, man, my head hurts. My ears hurt. My eyes hurt!"

Sean dusted himself off and got up, too. The two friends were alone on the side-walk.

"Wait," said Jeff, glancing around. "Where's the guy?" He looked up and down and all around Main Street. "The guy in the white coat. I think I saw him outside my house this morning. And he had some kind of big vegetable . . . "

"Never mind him," said Sean, shaking his head. "We're lucky we didn't get zapped to death with nuclear-powered X-rays. Now, come on. Put your helmet back in the box and let's go."

"I guess." Jeff continued to look up and down the street. "It was a cabbage, I think. Big leaves."

Jeff slipped off the chin strap of his Cosmic Boy Space Helmet and pulled.

"Ouch!" A sharp pain went through his head.

The helmet wouldn't budge. Jeff tugged again. It hurt more and still wouldn't move. "Sean, it's stuck on my head. Do something!"

Sean chewed his lip. "Well, I could sing the Cosmic Boy theme song and you could fly around. I don't remember all of it, though."

"Cut it out!" Jeff yelled, pulling again. "This is serious!"

But Sean sang what he knew.

> *No evil ploy,*
> *No scheme or trick,*
> *Can stop the Boy*
> *Known as Cosmic!*
> *Space Ahoy! Cosmic Boy!*

"I can't remember the rest," said Sean.

"Thanks a lot." Jeff gave his friend a nasty look. The gray plastic helmet felt strange on his head. But it was really on tight now. "I can't go to school like this."

Sean started toward school. "It looks okay. Sort of. Straighten your antennas, though. They're bent."

Jeff slumped along behind Sean. "Maybe I'll be lucky, and no one will say anything."

"Hey, everybody, look at Jeff!" shouted Mike Mazur when Jeff and Sean walked into the main hall of W. Reid Elementary

School. "He's got a toy space helmet on his head!"

Running up the hall behind Mike were Liz Duffey and Sean's sister, Holly.

Liz raised her eyebrows when she saw Jeff. "You must be the new kid. Welcome to Earth!"

Jeff smiled a fake smile under his helmet. "Sean jammed it on my head and now I can't take it off without taking off my ears, too. And now my head is itchy."

"Do you get cable on that thing?" asked Mike.

"Not funny," said Jeff.

Mike examined the gray plastic blinking helmet closely. "You know, it's amazing when you think about it. The brain is this big mushy thing sitting right there behind your forehead."

Sean nodded. "It's a lot neater that way. If your brain were on the outside, stuff would get stuck to it all the time."

"Especially in all those wrinkles," said Mike.

"It would probably hurt to iron them, though," Jeff said.

"But at least they'd look neat," said Sean.

"STOP IT!" cried Liz, slapping her hands over her ears. "You guys are shorting out my brain!"

Brrrrng! The morning bell rang.

"Thank you!" said Liz, heading off down the hall.

Jeff followed his friends to his classroom. *Zzzz!* went his helmet. His forehead blinked. His antennas twirled. He got some strange looks, even from the kindergartners.

"Maybe you could wear a turban or something," said Mike. "Maybe a chef's hat."

"They don't make hats that big," said Sean, heading for his classroom. "See you at tryouts, Cosmic Boy!" He and Mike went into their classroom across the hall.

Jeff shook his head and turned to Holly and Liz. "This isn't going to work. Everybody's going to ask me dumb questions."

"That's because you look super smart, Jeff," said Holly as they swung into their room. "By the way, do you know what's for lunch today?"

"No!" Jeff slumped into his seat in front of Holly and next to Liz. The other kids in the class giggled at him. His lights flickered. His head itched.

"Play tryouts are next period, Jeff," a boy said.

Jeff tried to smile. "I'm starting early."

Mrs. Carbonese, their white-haired teacher, looked up from her desk. "We're not landing planes here, Jeff. Please stop blinking."

"Yes, Mrs. Carbonese." Jeff tried to turn off the lights just as the PA system crackled to life.

"Ahem!" boomed the voice of Principal Bell. "As you know, this morning we are holding tryouts for *The Wizard of Oz*, delightfully updated for our modern times. Mrs. Carbonese will direct and my ac-

cordion and I will provide the music!"

Mrs. Carbonese smiled shyly at the class.

"Dancing astronauts, musical aliens," the principal went on. "There are parts for everyone!"

Liz shook her head and whispered to Jeff and Holly. "I'd like to see the Zoners get up on that stage. Now *that* would be interesting."

"And scary," whispered Holly. "Can you imagine Mrs. C. as a singing space woman?"

"Or Principal Bell doing his accordion thing. Talk about a musical alien!" said Liz.

Bweeeep! A sound came from somewhere.

"Jeff," said Mrs. Carbonese, looking up, "you're beeping."

Jeff frowned and adjusted his controls. "That wasn't me, was it?" That sound reminded him of the strange man that morning. He was sure the man in the bushes and the man with the X-ray machine were the same. And then there was the cabbage. What was that all about?

Jeff sighed. No, this wasn't going to be a normal everyday kind of day. It was going to be the other kind of day — weird.

Then, as Mrs. Carbonese went to the blackboard, Jeff saw something in the hallway just beyond the door.

A flash of white? A white coat?

"Name the American president during the Civil War," Mrs. Carbonese said, scraping a nib of chalk across the blackboard.

Bzzzzt! Jeff's helmet buzzed accidentally as he tried to see out into the hall.

"Your head just made a noise, Jeff," Mrs. Carbonese said. "Does that mean you know the answer?"

"It's the guy in the long white coat!" Jeff blurted out.

Mrs. Carbonese frowned. "No, actually, the president usually wore a long black coat. There is a famous memorial to this great man. Where is it?"

"At the X-ray place!" Jeff said, squinting into the hall to see more.

"No, no," said the teacher. "One final clue. What famous thing did he wear on his head?"

"A cabbage!" Jeff cried, rising from his seat.

"It is clear you haven't been studying," Mrs. Carbonese mumbled.

Bweeeep!

That sound! It came from the hall.

"It's him! He's there!" shouted Jeff, stumbling between the desks and out of the classroom.

"Jeff Ryan, take your seat!" Mrs. Carbonese said.

But he couldn't. The man in the white coat was standing in the shadows near the end of the hall. He seemed to have that leafy cabbage with him again.

"Who are you?" Jeff asked as he approached the shadows.

Then the man stepped into the light.

"No!" A jolt of horror struck Jeff as he realized something. "But . . . you're not holding a cabbage! It's your . . . *head!* You've got a cabbage . . . for a head!"

Toys in the Attic

"**Y**ou!" the man with the cabbage head began. "You have something of mine, and — "

Brnnng! The bell rang and the hall filled instantly with students.

"Tryouts!" shouted Sean, dashing from his classroom and nearly knocking Jeff down again. "To the auditorium!"

Jeff jumped back quickly and turned around. The man with the large green cabbage for a head had disappeared.

Jeff's own head ached and throbbed. The Cosmic Boy helmet was pinching his ears. "I don't get it. What's going on here? Who *is* that guy? *What* is that guy?"

Liz came out of the classroom with Holly. She gave Jeff a look. "Jeff, you really should have known the answers to those questions Mrs. C. was asking."

"Questions? But didn't you see that guy? He was . . . *different* . . ." Jeff stammered, then he stopped. Wait. Maybe he didn't see what he thought he saw. Or hear what he thought he heard.

"Plus you have that brain helmet, Jeff," said Holly. "It's supposed to make you look smarter. Anyway, come on. Tryouts."

Jeff followed his friends into the auditorium. On the floor in front of the stage was a long table filled with costumes and makeup. Standing in the middle of the stage was a large painted box with a curtain in front of it.

"Cool!" said Sean, walking over with Mike. "Behind that curtain is where the great and powerful Oz will sit. That's the part I want."

"But Jeff's already got the helmet," said Mike. "He's halfway there."

Jeff shook his helmeted head. Halfway crazy, maybe. He turned to his friends. "I think there's an alien — "

Woooooooo! Mrs. Carbonese blew hard into a silver whistle she always wore around her neck. "Silence, please!"

Zzzzt! Bzzz! Whrrr! Nnnn! went Jeff's helmet.

Mrs. Carbonese jerked around. "Jeff Ryan, is that your noisy head again? I'm afraid you'll have to wait in that box behind the curtain until I call for you."

Jeff slumped his shoulders and walked up the stage steps to the box with the curtain in front.

But when Jeff pulled aside the curtain, there he was! The man! The alien! With the cabbage-shaped head, all green and leafy!

His legs were crossed. At the ends of his legs were, not green shoes, but green feet!

"Ahhhhh!" cried Jeff, stumbling backward.

"Oh, what now?" said Mrs. Carbonese.

"Jeff, these interruptions are hurting your chances of getting the part you want."

"You have it!" the creature suddenly whispered to Jeff. His voice was raspy and deep. In the middle of his head were two enormous yellow eyes with red veins running through them.

"You have it!" the alien man repeated.

"The part of the Wizard?" asked Jeff.

"No, the Mezmo Head!" the alien said.

"The part of the Mezmo Head?" said Jeff.

The curtain moved and Sean and Mike came over to where Jeff was standing. "Hey, Jeff, what's going on — whoa! Great costume! What part are you?" Sean said to the creature in the chair.

"Cool lettuce head," said Mike, peering over Sean's shoulder at the stranger.

"I think it's a cabbage," said Sean. "Those veins give it away. My mom bought one once but I didn't like the way it tasted or — "

"STOP IT!" cried the alien, getting angry. He turned to Jeff and pointed a

24

long, greenish finger at him. "You have the Head in your house and I want you to bring it to me! Now!" He rolled his big yellow eyes at Jeff. "Do it, or I'll — " Then the alien jerked his big green head at Jeff.

Bweeeep! came a sound from the alien's head. The creature stood up.

Jeff's helmet started buzzing and sparking. "Let's get out of here!" he cried, bolting from the stage. Sean and Mike jumped after him as the green-headed alien emerged from the box.

"Yikes!" cried Holly, grabbing Liz by the arm. "That guy's costume is a little too real!"

"Who's he? The wicked alien of the east?" gasped Liz. She hurtled out into the hallway after her friends.

Bweeeep! the alien screeched again. He leaped from the stage into the hall after them.

"Children, behave," said Mrs. Carbonese.

"I want my head!" the alien cried.

"Whoa! And he's got such a big one already!" yelled Mike. "Split up!" He and Holly ducked into a classroom as Jeff, Sean, and Liz raced down the main hall to the front of the school.

Slap! Slap! The alien's large green feet slapped the floors behind them. The halls echoed loudly.

"He's still after us!" cried Liz. "We've got to get out of here now!"

Jeff's helmet wagged back and forth as he ran. His mind raced as he tried to make sense of what was happening. "He wants something at my house! Some kind of head. The answer is there! Maybe my mom and dad can help us!"

While Mike and Holly stayed at school, Jeff and the others rushed out the front doors, crossed Main Street, and raced down Birch Street to his house. The satellite dish on the roof wasn't moving.

"Your parents aren't home," Liz said, slowing to catch her breath.

Jeff quickly opened the door and the

three friends dived through, locking it behind them. Jeff looked out. "I don't see him. Maybe we lost him."

Then he turned to his friends. "Come on with me. We've got to check something out." He began to climb the stairs, but didn't go left into his room. He went right. Past his parents' room. Then right again.

"Where are you going?" asked Liz, following close behind him.

Jeff stopped at the door to the attic.

"I've never been in this part of your house," Sean said. "Is this the entrance to your dad's office?"

Jeff breathed deeply. "I think so. I've never gone farther than this door."

Errch! The attic door opened with a little squeak. Inside was a set of shiny metal stairs with little white lights running up the sides.

"I hope you know not every house has secret rooms like this," said Liz, following Jeff slowly up the metal stairs.

At the top of the stairs was a solid metal

slab. A digital keypad was set in the middle of it. In big red letters across the door was written DANGER.

The keypad beeped as Jeff tapped in some numbers. "One-two-two-eight-eight-five."

"How did you know that?" asked Sean.

"A voice in my brain told me," Jeff said.

"I'd like to hear that voice the next time I have a math test," Sean whispered to Liz.

Vrrrrt! The metal door slid aside, showing a vast room, glowing and twinkling with computer lights and dozens of TV screens. Stenciled on everything was *Property of U.S. Government.*

Through a skylight in the ceiling they could see the big satellite dish.

"Awesome!" gasped Sean. "This is where your dad works?"

"It's a total high-tech communications center," said Liz. "I think."

A secret room in his own house, Jeff thought. Why did his parents keep so many secrets from him?

Jeff ducked under the door so he wouldn't catch his Cosmic Boy helmet. He crossed the room and stood before a small silver panel on the wall. He tapped numbers into its keypad. "Zero-two-one-zero-nine-zero. It's that voice again."

Vrrrrt! The panel opened. And there it was.

A yellow dome rested on a stand. The dome had fins flying up the back and a long antenna coiling out of the top. On each side of the antenna were silver spoon-shaped panels catching the light as they turned. There were fancy silver nozzles, too.

"It's a helmet!" gasped Jeff.

"It's a helmet, all right," agreed Sean. "But it's way cooler than yours!" He read the letters along the rim. *"Zaldoonian Mezmo Head."*

"That's what he wants!" gasped Jeff.

"And now — I have it!" cried a raspy voice.

The three friends turned. There he was,

the cabbage-headed alien, at the bottom of the stairs.

His greenish leafy head pulsed as he spoke. "I am Klatoo, a Mezmo from the planet Zaldoon. And that is my official Mezmo Head. It's a mind control helmet. My ship went down last night and I lost the Head. I heard the buzzing at the X-ray place and thought my helmet might be in there. Then, I picked up signals from your brain. So I knew the Mezmo Head was here!"

"Wow, thanks for the explanation," said Sean. "It's pretty complete."

The alien smiled. "I have studied earthlings. They always want to know things like that." Suddenly he rolled his giant eyeballs again and snatched the Mezmo Head right off its stand.

"No!" cried Jeff. "You can't have it!"

"Now," said Klatoo, grasping the complicated device, "I shall conquer the world!"

Just then, a loud, thundering sound filled the air!

THONKA! THONKA! THONKA!

Jeff's whole house shuddered. The floor quaked. The windows rattled.

"A helicopter is circling the house!" said Liz.

"It's my mom and the U.S. Army!" cried Jeff, looking out the window. "They'll get you!"

"Pish-posh!" Klatoo snarled, putting the sparking, whirring helmet on his head. "I shall easily defeat them."

Before the kids could make a move, Klatoo leaned out the window and fired a jagged purple beam from the helmet's fancy silver nozzle.

BA-ZOOOSH! The helicopter suddenly dipped and spun around. Then it began flying figure eights over the Ryans' front yard.

"Get dizzy!" Klatoo snarled. Then he slowly floated out the window and over the house.

Jeff blinked. He shook his itchy head. "Did I just give the Mezmo Head helmet to that guy?"

"Uh, I don't think he's really a guy," Sean said. "His name is Klamez from Motoo, or something. And I think you just gave him, like, the ultimate power in the universe!"

"Oh, man," Jeff groaned. "This day is not going well."

"Come on, guys," said Liz. "Klatoo is floating toward the center of town. We've got to follow him."

The three kids dashed from the house and down the sidewalk. But when they reached Main Street, they stopped and stared.

Standing in the middle of the street was

a giant green tower, rising hundreds of feet from the ground. A large saucer-shaped thing lay flat across the top, like a hat.

"This is new," said Jeff.

"I didn't notice it this morning," mumbled Sean. "It sure changes the skyline."

"Hey, you guys, wait up!" cried a distant voice.

The three kids turned to see Holly and Mike running over to them, out of breath.

"We were at school," said Holly, staring up at the tower. "But then all the teachers and parents got strange. Well, stranger."

"Yeah, and now I guess we know why," added Mike, gaping at the new thing on Main Street. "Do you think someone's trying to take over? Or would that be too weird?"

"Klatoo is our leader!" someone yelled.

Suddenly a large crowd of grown-ups marched out onto Main Street. It looked like the entire adult population of Grover's Mill.

"We're doomed! We're doomed!" Mike

cried. "It's too late. They've already taken over! All is lost! Our lives are finished!"

"Calm down, Mike." Holly looked over at her friends. "Mike wants the part of the Cowardly Lion. He's practicing."

"But it does look pretty bad," said Jeff.

In the crowd were Rob and Bob Dunk, the Double Dunk Donut Den twins, selling pastries out of big boxes.

"Klatoo Krullers! Mezmo Muffins! Jelly Zaldoons!" they called out with glee.

Mike blinked. "Hmmm. Food. Well, maybe it's not *so* bad."

The crowd began chanting.

Klatoo is a Mezmo from Zaldoon,
He is and was!
Klatoo wants to conquer Earth real soon,
Oh, yes, he does!

"I sure don't like the sound of that!" Jeff said.

At the end of the long parade, Klatoo himself appeared, being carried on a portable throne like some kind of king.

Liz shook her head and searched the crowd. "This is creepy. At least my mom hasn't gone nuts for the alien."

"Nuts for the alien!" cried a voice. "Get your nuts for the alien here!"

Liz wheeled around to see her mother strolling through the crowd selling little bags of nuts.

"Now Klatoo has gone too far!" snarled Liz. "Taking over my mom is just too much!"

The silver nozzles on the alien's amazing Mezmo Head mind control helmet were whizzing around. They pointed at people and shot green beams at them.

Zaaap! The beams hit everyone in the same spot — right on the tops of their heads! Everyone marched faster when the green beams hit them.

"Klatoo is too-too-rific!" someone yelled.

"Wow, that beam really works," said Holly.

"He's zapping their brains!" Sean cried

out. "He wants us all to be his mind slaves! He wants us to do what he thinks! He wants to rule our world!"

"And I let him get the helmet," Jeff muttered. He was quiet for a while. "We can't just wait for him to take over. We have to do something."

Suddenly Klatoo held up a green hand. The parade stopped. Everyone looked into his big yellow eyes and smiled big smiles at him as he stepped down slowly from his porta-throne.

"Look at the Zoners," said Liz. "This is too gross."

Klatoo strode across the street to the kids, his large green feet slapping the pavement. *Slap! Slap!* He stared at the kids. His helmet sparked.

"What do you think of my tower?" the leafy alien asked them in his raspy voice. "Wait, don't tell me! I'll just read your minds!" The thick veins on his forehead twitched. "Oh! Planning to overthrow me, are you? Why, you're just children! On

Zaldoon, children are . . . pish-posh!"

"Pish-posh?" said Liz. "Is that a technical alien term?"

Klatoo only grinned a grim grin. The crowd closed around him and lifted him over to the giant green tower. He floated up slowly and disappeared inside the saucer at the top.

"One, two — Klatoo!" someone cheered. "Three, four — control us more!" With that, the crowd jerked away stiffly down Main Street. A moment later, the five kids were alone.

"This is major depressing," said Liz. "An alien has singlehandedly taken over our town since breakfast."

"Yeah," said Sean. "What are the odds?"

A sinking feeling hit Jeff, too. "I gave Klatoo the Mezmo Head. Now he's the most powerful alien in the world. And it's all my fault."

"It's okay, Jeff," said Sean, patting him on the shoulder. "We'll figure something out. We'll use our heads. Our brains are crammed with ideas, right?"

"Hey," said Holly, her face brightening. "Maybe that's why Klatoo can't control kids. Our brains are too filled up with stuff to do, thoughts and things. You know, pish-posh."

KA-SHOOMBA! A crater suddenly exploded out of the sidewalk right next to the five kids.

"Yikes!" screamed Mike, glancing up at the saucer. "He's shooting his head at us!"

At the top of the tower Klatoo adjusted his Mezmo Head helmet for another shot. "Two degrees left . . . "

"Watch out!" cried Liz. "That helmet's not just for mind control. It's for mind blowing up! Run, he's gonna blast us!"

The five friends scrambled across the street to the only open door they could find, the door of the X-Rays Я Us Medical Clinic.

Zzzzzt! went the X-ray machine.

"I'm not going in there again!" cried Jeff.

"Dive, or die!" yelled Sean, pushing Jeff ahead of him. Jeff tripped headfirst into the clinic, catching his foot on a work table. He fell toward the enormous X-ray machine.

BLAMMO! Klatoo's beam blasted the roof, tore through the ceiling, and exploded on the machine, just as Jeff fell.

ZZZZZZZZZZZZZ!

A sharp beam from the X-ray machine hit Jeff squarely in the center of his Cosmic Boy helmet.

The room filled with a million volts of energy.

So did Jeff's head.

The Power of Power!

The room darkened with thick clouds of blue smoke. A moment later, it cleared.

"Jeff, are you okay?" asked Sean, picking himself up from the floor and stumbling over to Jeff. "You've got a very weird look on your face."

"Not to mention the very weird shine coming from your head," added Mike, pointing to Jeff's plastic Cosmic Boy cap. "Your helmet! It's . . . glowing!"

Jeff reached up and touched the tips of his antennas. *Zzzzz!*

"Ouch! I got a shock!" Jeff blinked. "I feel . . . sort of strange. Did you see what just happened? It's like all the energy in the galaxy zapped into my head at the same time!"

"Your head must feel kind of crowded," said Holly, rubbing her elbows where she fell.

Jeff stretched his jaw and bent his neck "I can hear stuff, faraway stuff. And if I close my eyes, I can see . . . I think it's . . . TV."

"Wow, can you get cable now?" asked Mike. "What's on?"

"Wait . . . I . . . I can see through these walls right into the street!" Jeff went on. "I guess I sort of have X-ray vision! I can even see what Klatoo is up to at this exact moment. And, *sniff, sniff,* I can . . . smell stuff . . . Whew! What is *that?*"

"Probably your fried brain," said Liz. "That cannot have been good for you. I mean, look at you. Your head is practically on fire!"

Jeff tingled all over. His brain buzzed with energy and millions of thoughts, ideas, plans. For the first time in his life, things seemed crystal clear. Yes, Grover's Mill *was* the center of intergalactic weirdness. No doubt about that.

"I know!" Jeff blurted out. "Yes! I know that, too! And that and that, too!" His brain easily answered thousands of questions that had bothered him for years. Like, why do we yawn?

"Wow! That X-ray machine beamed an energy stream right to the center of my brain," Jeff said. "And I know everything!"

"What are X-rays anyway?" asked Holly.

Everyone shrugged. Except Jeff.

"X-rays are electromagnetic radiation created when electrons of very high energy bombard matter!" Jeff blurted out. "I'm pretty sure."

Sean's eyebrows went up. "Well, the X-rays zapped you, pal. They zapped you good."

"Sean is right," said Holly. "All that energy in you? We'd better get you to a doctor now."

Zzzzt! went the Cosmic Boy helmet.

"I guess," Jeff nodded. Then he jerked his head up. "But, first, I feel a strange need to . . ."

Jeff leveled his gaze at Mike. He blinked. His eyes seemed hot. Sparks shot off the antennas on his head. Then Mike began to rise in the air. Jeff stared and Mike started to spin in a circle.

"Incredible!" gasped Sean, an amazed smile spreading across his face. "Unbelievable!"

"Hey!" cried Mike. "Can I come down now?"

"Hmm," said Jeff, with a frown. "Strangely, I don't seem to know how to do that. I only know how to make you go — faster!"

"Whoa!" cried Mike, bumping faster and faster as he whipped around the ceiling.

While Mike was spinning, Liz's eyes grew wider and wider. She stepped over to the X-ray machine, then looked up at Jeff. "You're right," she said slowly. "The blast must have channeled incredible energy

right to the center of your brain. Jeff, you have super powers!"

"I know," Jeff said to her, still watching Mike.

"No, Jeff," Liz went on, "I mean you're different now. Like guys in costumes in comic books. You're a — superhero!"

Sean was wide-eyed, too, as Mike spun faster and faster. "It's true, Jeff. You do have powers. It's what I've always wanted. It's what everybody's always wanted!"

"I feel kind of sick up here," Mike groaned.

Holly gasped. "Jeff, that blast made you Cosmic Boy. You're the answer to our problem!" The others nodded.

Jeff listened, his eyes still fixed on how he was making Mike fly on the ceiling. *Cosmic Boy.* The words sounded magical. His new name. He remembered playing Cosmic Boy when he was young. A grin spread across his face. "Yes!"

"You're our hero," said Sean. "There's nothing you can't do. Cabbage heads? Ha!

You can take out aliens easy. Remember the call. Ahoy! Cosmic Boy!"

Zzzzz! Jeff's helmet screeched.

"Shhh! I'm picking up a signal!" He cupped his hands behind his ears, still watching Mike going around and around. "I hear Klatoo! He's talking to someone named King Greblak on Zaldoon. Klatoo's saying he's going to erase the minds of everyone in Grover's Mill. Greblak is telling him to hurry. He sounds mad. He wants to invade Earth . . . by tonight!"

"Only aliens would think of that!" said Holly.

Jeff cocked his head again. "Klatoo's going to tell them when to send more spaceships!"

"We can't let him do this," Liz said. "We have to stop Klatoo before he sends that message. We have to stop that invasion!"

Jeff lowered his gaze to the circle of friends. "Yes . . . it is up to us!"

Thud!

Mike fell to the floor. Hard.

Cosmic Boy!

"To the alien tower!" cried Sean. "Let's get Zaltoo from Kladoon!"

Mike sprang up from the floor, rubbing his shoulder. "Rev up your head, Jeff, and get him!"

"Yeah!" said Holly. "We're taking back our town!"

Jeff watched his friend bolt from the X-ray clinic and rush the enormous alien tower that rose hundreds of feet over Grover's Mill. They were very excited. But suddenly he wasn't sure about anything. "Uh, guys? Wait a minute. Don't we need a plan?"

Sean stopped and turned. "Don't waste

your incredible brain on that. I've already got a plan."

"You do?" asked Liz, a surprised look on her face.

"Sure," said Sean. He smiled. "We march up there and Jeff zaps him with his new head. It'll be great."

Mike slapped Sean a high-five. "Great plan."

Holly smiled. Liz shrugged.

Terrific, thought Jeff. His friends were all counting on him. As if he was the only chance they had. Well, maybe he was. He took a deep breath. He adjusted his knobs. *Zzzzt!* "Okay, I guess I'm ready."

He joined his friends, and they ran up to the base of the giant alien tower.

Thooop! The doors of a modern-looking elevator opened. It was all velvet inside. The kids piled in and the elevator began to rise.

Weee-ooo-weee-ooo! Musical sounds floated all around them.

"The way I see it," said Sean, starting to use his hands a lot, "we scope out the place, see what the alien guy is up to, then our boy takes him out. Zap and pow!" He slapped his fist into his palm. He nudged Jeff and smiled.

Liz frowned. *"Our boy?* You mean Jeff?"

Sean gave her a look as if she were from another planet. *"Jeff?* That was his old name. I'm talking about Cosmic Boy here. The Antenna Avenger, Buzz Brain, the Capped Crusader, the Domed Defender, Electrified Enforcer, the — "

"Sean!" cried Holly. "You don't have to run through the whole alphabet. We get the idea."

"Somebody's gotta manage the kid," Sean said. He nudged Jeff. "Right, Cosmic Boy?"

Jeff's helmet sparked and sizzled. Klatoo's futuristic Mezmo Head helmet was much scarier-looking than his own. It had way more knobs and nozzles than his own plastic toy. Sure, Jeff could lift people up in the air and maybe some other cool things. But would it be enough?

Thooop! The elevator doors opened and the five kids stepped out. Big windows on each side of the tower looked down on Main Street.

"Incredible," Liz said. "I always wanted to look out over Grover's Mill."

"Too bad it's from an alien tower," said Holly.

Slowly the kids turned to see a large room. In the center was a silver chair with its back to them. A green leafy bulge was visible over the top.

Weee-ooo-weee-ooo! Music rose from behind the chair.

"It's Klatoo!" whispered Sean.

Against the far wall was a giant shimmering screen.

"Wide-screen TV!" whispered Mike. "Do you think *he* gets cable?"

Pfft! The screen flickered and two alien heads appeared.

Liz gulped. "Two heads, one body!"

"Ah! King Greblak!" announced Klatoo from the chair. "Your kingly heads are looking very ripe today."

One head smiled back. "Well, thank you, Klatoo. I try to keep my leaves moist and — "

"Silence!" snapped the other head. He turned to the screen. "Klatoo, you've got two hours to conquer their minds!"

"Yes, my king, I will let you know when — "

"Just do it!" snapped the second head.

Pfft! The screen went dark.

"That one head has a bad temper!" said Holly.

Suddenly the chair spun around and there sat Klatoo. On his lap was something that looked like a futuristic accordion.

"So!" he said in a raspy voice. "The boy with the bowl on his head and his friends. You dare to confront me? I'm impressed."

Klatoo set his accordion on the floor and

rose. "I'd offer you all a seat, except that I lost some furniture yesterday, along with my helmet. In any case, welcome to my penthouse overlooking the first Zaldoonian Earth Colony!"

"Zaldoonian Earth Colony?" scowled Sean.

Jeff didn't like the sound of it, either. "We saw King Greblak — " he started.

"Where?" Klatoo whirled on his heels. His green face went pale. "Is he here already? Did you see him? I'm not ready for King Greblak yet!" Then he glared at Jeff. "Do not utter his kingly name. It's your fault I'm late with my mission!"

"Me?" said Jeff. "It's my fault?"

"You and your helmet!" Klatoo sputtered, thrusting his finger at Jeff. His own helmet went nuts, whirring and buzzing and blinking faster and faster and louder and louder. The veins on his big leafy head quivered and twitched.

"Bweeep!" the alien finally howled. Then he breathed deeply a few times and his

sputtering helmet died down to a low hum.

"Late with your mission?" said Sean. "That's nothing. Cosmic Boy is going to stop you cold! Show him, Jeff. Fly around."

Jeff shut his eyes and focused his brain waves.

Zang! Zang! Zang! Light blue beams sprayed wildly off his head.

"Ow!" cried Mike, grabbing his arm and diving for the floor. "Why is it always me?"

Crash! A lamp fell over. An ashtray broke.

"Sorry," said Jeff. He shut his eyes tighter. Slowly he began to rise into the air.

"See? See?" said Sean. "Our boy is tough."

"Ah, you can fly. Nice. But can you do this?" Klatoo looked down over Grover's Mill. His Mezmo Head helmet lit up.

Zzzzt! Kkkkk! Wrrrr! Suddenly the perfectly straight Main Street began to turn. It bent itself into a perfect S, right down the middle of town!

Jeff touched down. "I can't do that. No way."

A smile stretched across the alien's mouth as he adjusted a knob or two on his head. "Just a small show of my power. Let's meet in one hour, to settle this for good."

"You're on!" cried Sean. "One hour! Our boy will be ready for you!"

The alien smirked. "Wear something you'd be caught dead in. Because you will be! Now GET OUT!"

A few minutes later, the five kids were in the elevator traveling down. "What just happened there?" asked Jeff. "Can anybody tell me?"

Sean beamed. "I just arranged for you to battle Mezmo the Zaldoon Head from Klatoo. Superhero against super alien. Just the two of you!"

"But you heard Klatoo," said Holly. "The others are on their way. Thousands of them."

"Millions, probably," offered Mike. "And

all of them with cabbage heads and buggy eyes."

Thoop! The doors opened and hundreds of creatures with green faces and bulging yellow eyes lunged at the kids!

"Aliens!" gasped Holly. "They're already here!"

Almost Aliens

The green-faced yellow-eyed creatures surrounded Jeff and his friends. They pointed their weapons at them and prepared to fire.

"Don't vaporize us!" said Sean, ducking behind his sister, Holly. "We'll do anything you say! We love Klamo the Toozal from Mezdoon!"

One of the creatures came toward them. It removed its green face.

"It's . . ." gasped Liz, "it's . . . a mask!"

The face underneath the mask smiled at Jeff.

"Mom!" said Jeff.

It was Mrs. Ryan! She was dressed in a

shiny black body suit and green gas mask.

Jeff saw the look in her eyes. "I know, Mom." He hung his helmeted head in shame. "I gave the alien your super brain helmet."

"It was his, anyway," said his mother. "We saw his saucer last night and fired at it. We always fire at saucers. We thought it crashed but all we found were a couple chairs and that strange helmet. It was only a matter of time before he came looking for it."

"In case you didn't know, Mrs. Ryan," said Sean, "the alien's name is Meztoo or something. He started controlling brains, but he can't do kid brains because we're too filled up with all kinds of neat stuff."

"How did you survive?" Mike asked.

"Our gas masks keep us safe," Mrs. Ryan said.

"But the worst part," said Jeff, "is that a whole bunch more like him are coming to take over."

Mrs. Ryan smiled, then turned to the

soldiers. "Troops, we've been waiting for this. Aliens want to take over? The official U.S. Government response is — ha!"

Snap! Snap! Mrs. Ryan snapped her fingers.

In an instant, soldiers rushed up and down the streets of Grover's Mill, setting up big barricades. Army trucks, tanks, and jeeps rumbled down every road and alley and took up positions around the alien tower. Thousands of eyes were trained on the saucer at the top.

"Boys and girls, I'd like to introduce Plan A!" said Mrs. Ryan. She smiled as she said this, pointing to the hills.

Rrrrrrr!

Fighter jets, dozens of them, headed in from the mountains north of town. Flying in battle formation, they made their way toward the giant alien tower.

Jeff's heart swelled with pride as the rumbling sound filled the sky. He crouched in front of Duffey's Diner with his friends. "You know," he said, "I'm sort of glad I don't have to use my powers, because I'm not really sure — "

BLAM! BOOM! KA-VOOSH! The jets began firing missiles at the alien tower, sending streams of black smoke shooting through the air!

Just then, the top of the saucer opened and Klatoo stuck out his Mezmo Head.

"He's coming out!" yelled Jeff.

"Perfect!" cried Sean. "One fried Mezmo Head coming up!"

"Blast that alien!" shouted Holly. "And keep Grover's Mill for the people!"

But as Jeff watched, he wondered if it was too soon to start celebrating.

KA-VOOSH! BOOM! BLAM!

It *was* too soon. Way too soon. All the missiles exploded in the air above the tower, and the energy from the blasts was sucked right down into Klatoo's helmet!

"Uh-oh!" gasped Mrs. Ryan, looking through binoculars. "Plan B, quick!"

Instantly, all the guns on all the tanks

and jeeps and trucks started pumping blast after blast at the tower!

BOOM-BOOM-BOOM!

Same thing! The big explosions were sucked right into Klatoo's Mezmo Head!

The alien's helmut sizzled with all the dark and powerful energy he had gotten from the missile and bomb explosions.

"He's even stronger now!" cried Liz.

"He's invincible!" cried Mike. "We're doomed! We'll be in his control by supper-time! It's too late! All is lost!"

Mrs. Ryan frowned. "Well, then — Plan C!" She dashed back to her jeep and snatched her combat phone. "I want the top-secret weapon! Yes, that's right! What? Oh, it is? When did that happen? Uh-huh? Oh, well, maybe next time. Bye-bye!"

"That didn't sound good," said Liz.

"What is the secret weapon?" asked Holly.

"It's a nuclear-powered negative proton beam that — " Mrs. Ryan stopped. "Wait!

It's top secret! Forget what I just said. And that's an order!"

Jeff knew what this was all leading to.

Him. By himself. Alone against the crazy alien.

Klatoo leaned over the top of the tower. His head buzzed wildly from its new power.

"It's no use, Mom," Jeff told his mother sadly. "Klatoo is super smart and powerful. And his creatures are on the way. Thousands like him."

"Millions!" said Mike. "Maybe billions!"

"They'll take over our minds," Jeff went on. "They'll make us all aliens in our own town."

A shudder ran through the troops of soldiers.

Mrs. Ryan looked at Jeff. "I didn't want to resort to Plan D, but now there's no choice."

"Excellent! There's still hope!" said Sean. "What's Plan D?"

Mrs. Ryan called her troops together. "Plan D. RUN FOR YOUR LIVES!"

"But M-M-M . . . Mom!" stuttered Jeff.

Within seconds the streets were empty. The army was gone. The tanks were gone, the trucks were gone, the jeeps and jets were gone.

Mrs. Ryan was gone.

The kids were alone.

Klatoo stared down from the giant alien tower. He began to laugh. He tapped a futuristic watch on his green wrist.

"Ten minutes, Cosmic Boy!"

He laughed some more. An ugly, alien laugh, that drifted down slowly, along with the *weee-ooo-weee-ooo* sounds of his accordion.

Showdown!

Sean turned to Jeff. "Can you do this? I mean, can you defeat the evil Mezmo-Headed dude?"

The lights on Jeff's plastic helmet blinked as he looked at Sean and the others. One after the other, each of his friends — Sean, Liz, Holly, Mike — gave him hopeful nods.

"I guess I can," said Jeff. "I mean, I'll try."

Sean beamed. "All right! The kid is turned on and ready for action!" He looked at the others. "See? What did I tell you?"

Mike frowned. "I still don't think we're going to make it this time. Those aliens are going to force us to listen to accordions all the time."

"Listen, guys," said Jeff. "We've got to short out Klatoo's head before he sends any more signals to the others."

"Short out?" said Holly. "How? You saw how his helmet sucked in that huge explosion. He's super smart *and* super powerful. I think maybe we'd better do like your mom. You know, Plan D?"

Jeff took a deep breath. "There's got to be a way to short circuit that helmet. He's probably just a normal everyday alien without it."

"Right!" said Liz. "Normal."

Suddenly Jeff's helmet buzzed and blinked and whirred as he stared at the giant tower. "Stand back!" he shouted. "A plan is beginning to form in my brain!"

"Go, Cosmic Boy!" Sean cheered. "A plan!"

Jeff shut his eyes tight and pinched his temples. Blue sparks flew off his helmet. His face glowed. His fingers felt electric.

"Yes . . . " said Jeff. "Good . . . okay . . . really? Got it!"

He turned to his friends. "There's only one way to stop Klatoo. Let's put on a show!"

"A show?" said Mike.

Liz was staring at Jeff. Suddenly her face brightened. "In school. The stage in the auditorium. Jeff, you've got something up your sleeve!"

Jeff smiled a little. "On my head, really." He adjusted the knobs on his helmet and straightened his antennas for the attack. "Yes, our school. Our turf."

VRRR! The top of the saucer began to open.

"Everybody back to school," said Jeff calmly. "Mike, you go to the kitchen."

"Cool," said Mike.

"And get me a cabbage. . . ." Jeff stopped and looked at Sean's head. "Better make it two cabbages. Sean, I need a roll of duct tape. Holly, lights. Liz, music."

Jeff's friends just stared at him.

"I'll explain it all when I get there," he said. "Now go!"

They went.

And as they went, Jeff felt as if big music were pounding in the air all around him. Not accordion music, but action music. He looked at the giant alien tower with the saucer at its summit.

The top was completely open now. Jeff's friends were rushing away up Main Street to school.

He was alone.

Battleground U.S.A., he thought, his plastic helmet still buzzing on his head. Grover's Mill was the first line of defense against the alien invasion of Zalmo from Klamez. Doontoo from Mokla. Oozal from Zemom. Whatever.

"First battleground," Jeff said to himself, turning his knobs to maximum. "Final showdown!"

Bong! The giant donut chimed the hour.

Sssss! The pancake pan hissed it, too.

Time was almost up.

Suddenly there he was, floating down to the street. Klatoo the alien. His leafy head fluttered in the breeze.

Slap! Slap! His large green feet slapped the ground. His large yellow eyes in his large green head stared at Jeff from under his large mind control helmet. "Now I will destroy you!" he growled.

Zzzzzt! A spark flared from the cone at the top of Klatoo's finned helmet. It slowly massed itself into a giant purple ball of energy.

Jeff braced himself as dust swirled up on the empty pavement. Klatoo shot his fireball at Jeff.

ZANNNNNNG! BLAM!

Jeff reeled backward as Klatoo's first blast zapped his twin wire antennas. "Oh, that hurts!"

But that blast was just a trick! When Jeff staggered back, Klatoo swung and jerked his head at his friends running toward the school.

KKKKK! VA-SHOOOM!

"Oh, no you don't!" Jeff cried out.

ZZZZ! Jeff's light blue bolt shot across the street and met Klatoo's purple ray in midair.

KA-BOONG! The two fireballs collided and exploded harmlessly in the air. But the blast sent both Jeff and the alien faltering backward. His friends disappeared safely around the corner.

WHAMMO! Another alien blast came quickly. Jeff leaped up off the street as Klatoo's shot hit near his sneakers, scorching them. *Hsssss!* It scorched them!

VLANG! KA-JOOM! The battle went on. Jeff kept trying to dodge the purple blasts. The only thing stopping the total destruction of Grover's Mill was Jeff's plastic helmet. And boy was it giving him a headache!

He floated over Duffey's Diner and hurled another blast. *BLAM!* It exploded at Klatoo's large green feet.

Suddenly the alien stopped. His Mezmo Head sputtered softly. "You are powerful, Cosmic Boy. Why not stop fighting and rule together? You can be the last human. We will be your Zaldoonian alien friends."

Jeff looked Klatoo right in his bulging yellow eyes. "I don't want to be the only human. I sort of like the way things are. My friends and stuff."

Klatoo's head sparked. "Then prepare to die!"

VLAMMO! A sizzling purple blast shot off the alien's helmet and screamed through the air at Jeff.

Jeff ducked and the beam whizzed past him. "I'm getting out of here!" He shot

another blue blast, then tore across the street and down School Road.

"I'll get you!" Klatoo shrieked. "King Greblak commands that I succeed! And I shall!"

VOONG! SHOOM! The sidewalk blasted apart behind Jeff as he raced through the doors of W. Reid Elementary. His friends were waiting for him.

"Did you get him good?" asked Sean. "Is he, you know, finished?"

Jeff chewed his lip. "Uh, not quite, but I think I slowed him down a little." He turned to Mike. "Cabbages?"

Mike handed him two leafy bundles.

"Duct tape?" said Jeff.

Sean tossed him a roll of shiny black tape.

Jeff smiled. "Props," he said, mysteriously. "Now to the auditorium!"

"Ahem! Not so fast!" boomed a voice from the shadows.

Principal Bell stepped out, his hands on

his hips. His eyes were glassy. "Klatoo is our leader and our friend!"

"Uh-oh, I've got to override Klatoo's thought beam with mine!" cried Jeff.

Zzzzz! He zapped Mr. Bell's brain.

"But . . ." the man protested. He blinked. "Klatoo is our enemy! We must stop him!"

"The whole alien cabbage-head army is coming!" Liz told him.

"Shocking!" Mr. Bell announced. "Grover's Mill is the loveliest of towns! It must survive!"

"I think we all agree about that." Jeff smiled when he thought of the next part. "But we need your help, Principal Bell."

The tall man folded his arms and stared down at Jeff. "*My* help, young man? Fighting the aliens? Hmmm. Yes, that would help my career. What can I do?"

"How musical are you, Mr. Bell?" asked Jeff. Then he beamed another thought beam into Mr. Bell's brain.

Everyone charged for the auditorium.

Suddenly — *KA-ZANG!* Klatoo the Mezmo Head blasted the front doors off the school!

"So, you've chosen the battleground!" said the raspy-voiced alien through his tight green lips.

Klatoo leaned forward and hurled a super-powered Mezmo energy bolt at Jeff! *KA — ZOW!*

Jeff quickly tossed the cabbage and the duct tape to Sean. Then he stuck out his hands and created a force field around himself. Klatto's energy bolt bounced off and hit a water fountain instead. Water sprayed all over the hall.

"*Heads* up, Klatoo!" Jeff snarled, hurling his own blue bolt of energy at the alien.

"There's a *brainy* suggestion," Klatoo retorted, sending another beam.

"I hope you don't *mind!*" Jeff said, floating to the ceiling and zapping back.

"Watch where you're *head*ed!" the alien

cried. Another purple bolt shot from his head.

Sean stopped outside the auditorium. "How long can they keep this up?"

"Not much longer I hope," said Liz, sliding down next to him. "It's making me mental!"

Klatoo the Destroyer

But the two helmeted super beings *could* keep it up! As the school blew apart, Jeff — otherwise known as Cosmic Boy — matched Klatoo the Evil Mezmo Head from Zaldoon blast for blast!

"I've been *think*ing of you!" said Klatoo. *KA-BOOM!*

"Here's a wave," said Jeff. "A *brain* wave!"

BA-ZANG!

"I've got an *idea* for you!" blurted Klatoo. *KROONCH!*

Jeff dodged the shot. "Your *mind* is a blank!"

BOOMF!

"I *think*, therefore I blast!" shouted the alien.

"STOP IT!" yelled Liz.

But they couldn't stop it. The energy was too great. Powerful fireballs blasted off the two great helmets. Whole chunks were being blown out of the school walls. It was a mess!

Skipping and dodging blast after alien blast, Jeff made his way to the auditorium.

"Jeff, get in here!" yelled Sean, dashing out into the hallway.

"Children everywhere!" Klatoo shouted, his head popping and buzzing. "I'll even up the odds." A purple fireball of energy started to form on his Mezmo Head. He aimed it at Sean. The air sparkled and sizzled.

"No!" screamed Jeff. "My friends aren't for frying!" He flew across the hall and took the blast meant for his best friend. He took it right in the antennas!

KA—ZZZZZZZZ!

Jeff's head jerked backward as the purple fireball hit. His antennas were as hot as . . . as . . . something really hot!

"Whoa! Barbecued head!" Sean gasped, flat on the floor. "Thanks, pal."

But the force of the blast knocked Jeff to the wall with a terrible crunch. He tried to fire one of his light blue beams back at the alien.

Fzzz-zzz. Sproing! A wire from his Cosmic Boy helmet whizzed down and dangled in front of his nose.

"No!" Jeff groaned. "My powers! My powers! They're . . . gone!"

At that exact moment Klatoo charged out of the shadows and rushed toward Jeff. "Prepare to die!" he cried, his lips growling into a grim grin.

"No!" shouted Liz. "Prepare to be entertained!" The auditorium doors burst open and Principal Bell and Mrs. Carbonese strutted out, both with accordions strapped on them. And both playing terribly. *Weee-ooo-weee-ooo!*

Klatoo turned to look at the two grown-ups. "Could it be? The sacred music of Zaldoon!"

In that half second, Jeff scrambled through the double doors and into the auditorium.

"Everybody!" he cried. "My helmet's busted. I need some help!"

Mike raced over and looked at the snapped wires on the Cosmic Boy helmet. "I can fix this. I just need some time."

Jeff glanced at the auditorium stage. "It's show time!"

KA-BOOM! The door burst open and Mr. Bell and Mrs. Carbonese raced in. "I don't think we play well enough for him!" cried the principal, dashing over and huddling in a distant corner.

"Sean, up here with me! Mike, fix my head!" Jeff called to his friends. "We've got to do this!" He jumped up on the stage and nodded to Holly and Liz. "Places everyone!"

The two girls dashed over to the light box and threw a big switch.

The auditorium was plunged into darkness.

Sean and Mike scrambled behind the box on the stage with the curtain in front.

Jeff grabbed the cabbages and the tape and dived through the curtains and onto the throne at the back of the box.

Mike stuck his hands through the back curtains, grabbed Jeff by the helmet, and began working on the wires. Sean poked his head through next to Jeff's. Everyone was in position.

WHAM! The rear auditorium doors swung open with a bang and Klatoo entered. His helmet sizzled and sparked in the darkened room.

"Where are you, earthling children?" the alien uttered, walking slowly down the center aisle.

"Lights!" yelled Jeff from inside the box.

FLINK! A bright hot spotlight shone down from the ceiling right on Klatoo's green face.

"Bweeeep!" he screeched. "I can't see!"

Whoosh! The curtains in front of the box on the stage were pulled aside. Sitting there in the dim light was Jeff. On his shoulder, poking through from behind, was Sean's head. Both of them were covered with large green cabbage leaves stuck on with duct tape.

They looked just like an alien. Just like —

"King Greblak!" Klatoo's wide yellow eyes grew wider and yellower. "You're . . . here?"

"Yeah," said Jeff. "I mean, yesssss!" he intoned in as deep a voice as he could.

Klatoo approached slowly. Liz and Holly kept the bright spotlight trained right on Klatoo. His big yellow eyes squinted at Jeff and Sean, trying to get a better look.

"But, King Greblak, why are you not dressed in the traditional Zaldoonian uniform?" the alien asked.

Jeff began to sweat. He felt the sweat

seeping down under his cabbage leaves.

"Are you saying you don't like my outfit?" Sean asked sweetly.

"No, no, my king!" Klatoo answered. "Forgive me, I — "

"Forgive you?" Jeff exploded. "But you haven't conquered Earth yet!"

Mike continued to fiddle with the damaged wires on Jeff's helmet.

Klatoo's yellow eyes blinked in the bright spotlight. "There are hands behind one of your wondrous heads, oh great one."

"Uh . . . " mumbled Jeff. "Uh . . . but enough about me! Why isn't Earth ready?"

Klatoo bowed his Mezmo Head. "The earthlings . . . they are mighty, King Greblak."

"We are?" yelled Sean from beneath his leafy disguise. "Yahoo! The cabbage dude thinks we're mighty! He thinks — " Sean stopped. Klatoo's big yellow eyeballs began to burn. "Ooops," said Sean quietly.

"Earthling children!" shrieked Klatoo.

"You dare to impersonate the great King Greblak of Zaldoon? You . . . pish-posh!"

KKKK! The alien's helmet began to pop and spark and sputter. It flared and flamed.

A huge fireball shot up from the Mezmo Head helmet at the same instant as Mike jumped up and shouted, "Jeff, your head is fixed!"

In a flash, Jeff bolted from the throne and fired his ultimate and final and ultra and mega Cosmic Boy blast!

KLA — BLAMMMMMMO!

Just Normal Weird

KA — WHOOOOOOOOM!

A ball of white-hot flame exploded in the auditorium of W. Reid Elementary School and blew out into the hallway.

Jeff's plastic helmet took the blast hard. It burst into a thousand pieces, and he went hurtling out of the auditorium at incredible speed.

"Ugh! Ouch! Umph! Whoa! *Crunch!*"

When the explosion died down, a lone figure staggered up the hall. "Ohhh! My Mezmo Head! I have failed! I have dishonored my great King Greblak!" Klatoo's futuristic Mezmo Head helmet was melted down and smoking on his leafy green head.

"Whew!" said Sean, crawling out into the hall. "What is that smell?"

"Burnt cabbage," muttered Liz, picking herself up from the floor next to Holly.

"It's Klatoo!" shouted Jeff, jumping up from the floor. "We zapped his head! We won! We shorted him out! We won!"

Suddenly — *RRRRRRRR!* An eerie sound penetrated the school from outside. Jeff and his friends ran out to the sidewalk and looked up.

"Whoa!" gasped Sean. "It's big!"

Big? It wasn't big. It was enormous! And round! With thousands of lights on it!

"Oh, no, a spaceship!" cried Mike. "We're doomed. We defeated Klatoo, but we're too late. His alien friends are here! All is lost!"

The enormous round spaceship billowed slowly out of the clouds like some special effect in a super-expensive Hollywood movie.

The ship hovered over Grover's Mill. The entire town grew dark in its shadow.

VRRRT! An opening appeared in the bottom of the hull. Piercing green light flooded from the opening onto the sidewalk in front of the school.

"It's going to fire!" yelled Holly. "Take cover!"

But Jeff didn't move. He knew what was going to happen. He watched as the light flared brighter and brighter. Then a single beam of green light shot down at Klatoo, the Mezmo Head from Zaldoon.

"Now he's going to get it," Jeff said to himself.

Klatoo floated up the beam and into the giant ship. He moaned the whole way up.

"It's taking him away!" shouted Holly.

Jeff could hear Klatoo being yelled at because he couldn't control the kids' brains. "Too full of stuff!" Jeff heard Klatoo plead. But it was no good. King Greblak was yelling really loud.

"Ahem!" Principal Bell stormed out of the school, his accordion still strapped on.

"If they are trying out for our play, I'm afraid tryouts are only for students from our school."

Sean raced over. "Hey, everybody! The song! I remember it now!" Sean sang as Mr. Bell played.

> *His fingers, they*
> *Command the stars*
> *From Pluto all*
> *The way to Mars*
> *Space Ahoy!*
> *Cosmic Boy!*

VOOOOOM! The spaceship left. It sucked up Klatoo's alien tower with the saucer on top. Main Street uncurved itself.

Jeff smiled at his friends. "I'm not Cosmic Boy anymore," he said, scratching his head for the first time since that morning. "But I'm sort of glad."

"Amazing," said Liz after it was all over. "We just can't get away from it, can we?

I mean, no matter what happens to it, Grover's Mill is here to stay."

"I always knew it would be," said Mike.

Jeff kept scratching his head. It felt so good. He looked down Main Street, straight once again. People were starting to fill the shops, the restaurants. Soon it would look just as it had that morning. "Maybe it's not so incredibly weird, after all."

Bong! The Double Dunk Donut Den's donut-shaped clock chimed the hour.

Sssss! Steam rose from Usher's House of Pancakes' giant pan into a cloudless sky.

A sky with no spacecraft in it. For now.

"Right, Jeff," said Sean. "Just normal everyday weird."

THE WEIRD ZONE

#8

BIZARRE EERIE HILARIOUS

Written and Directed by Tony Abbott

Just when things in Grover's Mill seem like normal weird, the ground starts to shake and large Tiki men start popping up all over town! Can the kids successfully battle the evil forces and restore the Zone?

Revenge of the Tiki Men!

THE WEIRD ZONE #8
by Tony Abbott

WZT1196